Dear Parent:
Your child's love of reading starts here!

Every child learns to read in a different way and at his or her own speed. Some go back and forth between reading levels and read favorite books again and again. Others read through each level in order. You can help your young reader improve and become more confident by encouraging his or her own interests and abilities. From books your child reads with you to the first books he or she reads alone, there are I Can Read Books for every stage of reading:

SHARED READING
Basic language, word repetition, and whimsical illustrations, ideal for sharing with your emergent reader

BEGINNING READING
Short sentences, familiar words, and simple concepts for children eager to read on their own

READING WITH HELP
Engaging stories, longer sentences, and language play for developing readers

READING ALONE
Complex plots, challenging vocabulary, and high-interest topics for the independent reader

ADVANCED READING
Short paragraphs, chapters, and exciting themes for the perfect bridge to chapter books

I Can Read Books have introduced children to the joy of reading since 1957. Featuring award-winning authors and illustrators and a fabulous cast of beloved characters, I Can Read Books set the standard for beginning readers.

A lifetime of discovery begins with the magical words "I Can Read!"

Visit www.icanread.com for information
on enriching your child's reading experience.

For Ezzy and Levon

DukE   Roxy   Buddy

I Can Read Book® is a trademark of HarperCollins Publishers.

Library of Congress Control Number: 2016936917
ISBN 978-0-06-235709-0 (trade bdg.)—ISBN 978-0-06-235708-3 (pbk.)

The artist used Adobe Illustrator to create the digital illustrations for this book.
Design by Erica De Chavez. Hand-lettering by James Horvath.

17 18 19 20 21 SCP 10 9 8 7 6 5 4 3 2 1 ❖ First Edition

James Horvath

Work, Dogs, Work

A Highway Tail

Max　　　Spot　　　Spike

HARPER

An Imprint of HarperCollinsPublishers

Fill up your cups;
today is a big day.
We've got miles and miles
of new road to lay.

Load up the trucks.

It's time to get moving.

There's a road out there

that needs some improving.

This road is old
and in need of repair.
We'll fix it right up
from here to there.

We'll need a bulldozer and a grader or two,

a steamroller,   a loader,

and a paving truck, too.

Bulldoze a path
and smooth it with graders.
No more bumps
from potholes and craters!

The steamrollers roll

heavy and slow.

They flatten and level

the dirt as they go.

Dump trucks rumble as

Duke makes the call:

"Head out to the quarry and

haul, dogs, haul!"

The rock quarry is where
we get all of our stone.
The dump truck fills up
in the rock-loading zone.

Huge quarry trucks

are too big for the street.

To move tons of rock,

these trucks can't be beat.

The dump trucks dump
straight into the hopper.
The paver spreads tar
until it looks proper.

Dump trucks deliver
load after load.
It will take lots of trips
to build this long road.

The road crew is busy

dropping orange cones.

They help keep us safe

in construction zones.

Stop, dogs, stop!

You have to wait here.

Go, dogs, go!

The road is now clear.

We can't go through here;
our trucks will get stuck.
It's mile after mile of
deep, sticky muck!

With hills on both sides,

Duke knows what to do.

"Get digging, dogs!

We must tunnel through!"

The rock is too hard

to dig our way through.

Time to bring in

the demolition crew!

Set the charges and
get out of there fast.

Shout, "Fire in the hole!" then

blast, dogs, blast!

Take cover now, stand clear,

make some room.

The tunnel blasts open

with a great, big

Clean up this rubble.

Let's haul it away.

Work, dogs, work!

There's more road to lay.

Now here we are

on the opposite side.

We'll need a tall bridge

at least four lanes wide.

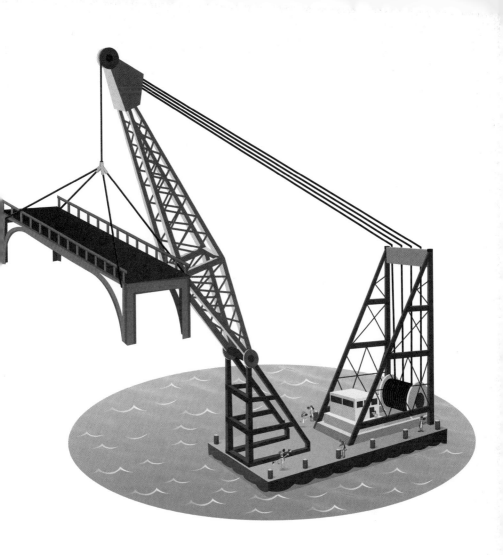

The barge crane is here
to lift up the sections.
We'll finish the job
if we follow directions.

Strong steel towers,

concrete, and cable

help to make our
bridge very stable.

The crew helps set up
some shiny road signs.
The last thing to do
is to paint all the lines.

The road runs for miles;

now the end is in reach.

From the city, through hills,

all the way to the beach.

We're finally finished.

It's been a long day.

Now get out in those waves and

play, dogs, play!